MR. BADGER AND MRS. FOX #2

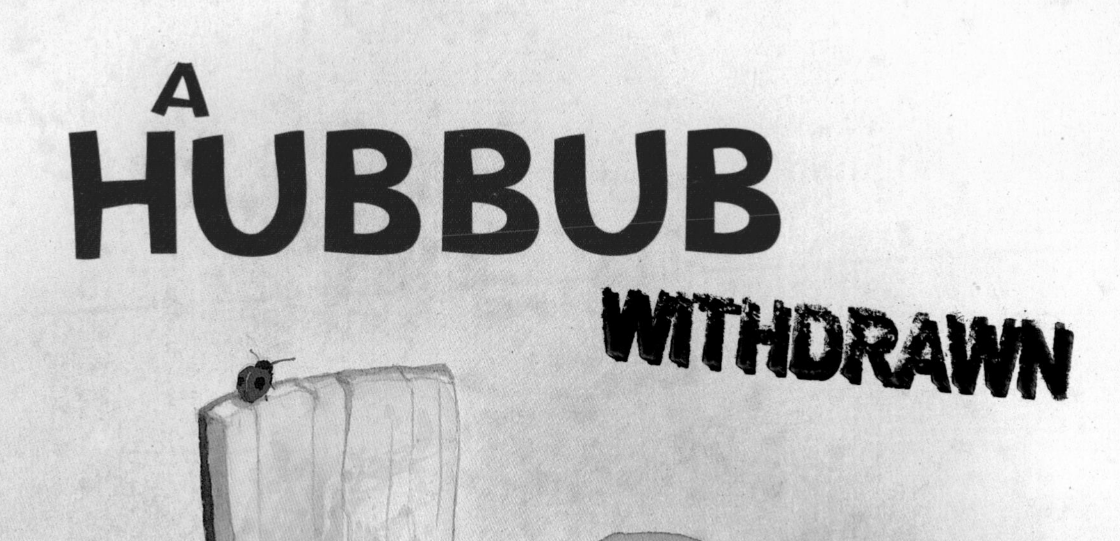

A HUBBUB

Brigitte LUCIANI & Eve THARLET

Graphic Universe™ • Minneapolis • New York

Thank you to Briac and to Jean-Marie B. for the inspiration. —E.T.

Story by Brigitte Luciani
Art by Eve Tharlet
Translation by Edward Gauvin

First American edition published in 2010 by Graphic Universe™.
Published by arrangement with MEDIATOON LICENSING - France.

Monsieur Blaireau et Madame Renarde
2/Remue-ménage

www.dargaud.com

Graphic Universe™
A division of Lerner Publishing Group, Inc.
241 First Avenue North
Minneapolis, MN 55401 U.S.A.

Website address: www.lernerbooks.com

Library of Congress Cataloging-in-Publication Data

Luciani, Brigitte.
[Remue-ménage. English]
A hubbub / by Brigitte Luciani ; illustrated by Eve Tharlet. — 1st American ed.
p. cm. — (Mr. Badger and Mrs. Fox ; 2)
"Published by arrangement with MEDIATOON LICENSING France."—T.p. verso.
Summary: Ginger the fox learns that, even though life with just her mother was very different, being part of a family can be a good thing, such as when some unwanted cats try to take over the children's clubhouse.
ISBN: 978-0-7613-5626-4 (lib. bdg. : alk. paper)
[1. Stepfamilies—Fiction. 2. Brothers and sisters—Fiction. 3. Badgers—Fiction. 4. Foxes—Fiction. 5. Cats—Fiction. 6. Toleration—Fiction.] I. Tharlet, Eve, ill. II. Title.
PZ7.7.L83Hub 2010
[Fic]—dc22 2010005714

Manufactured in the United States of America
2 - DP - 2/1/11

It's been a year to the day since you and your daughter landed in our burrow.
A fair wind blew us there!
A VERY fair wind.
And a few nasty hunters!
We'll have to thank them someday. Without them, we would never have met!
Yes. Without meaning to, they brought us good luck!
Even the children are happy together!
You're just a big dummy!
Look, the scaredy-cat is getting all scared.

You're full of hot air, **snot-snout!**
You're completely clueless, slug-brain!
Come on, Ginger, **go for it!**

You flea-filled carpet!
Striped doormat!
Fly doody!
Skunk fart!

Mind your language!

What's going on here?

Don't worry about it.
Everything's fine!

I only had my friends to practice on. But you can argue much better with a brother. It's **natural!**

Whew!
Lucky we were only on your first lesson.
Yeah. Papa hates it when we fight.

He's way too strict sometimes!
You and your mother just aren't used to it.

It's **no fun** getting surprised like that. We'd better go to our clubhouse.
Right. But first we have to decorate it a bit.

Yes! With a comfy chair!
And a storeroom for walnuts!
I'd like to have a little art studio.

That won't be easy.
But why not try?

I think we have a problem...

It's too **small!**

No it's not!
Look around! There's lots of room...

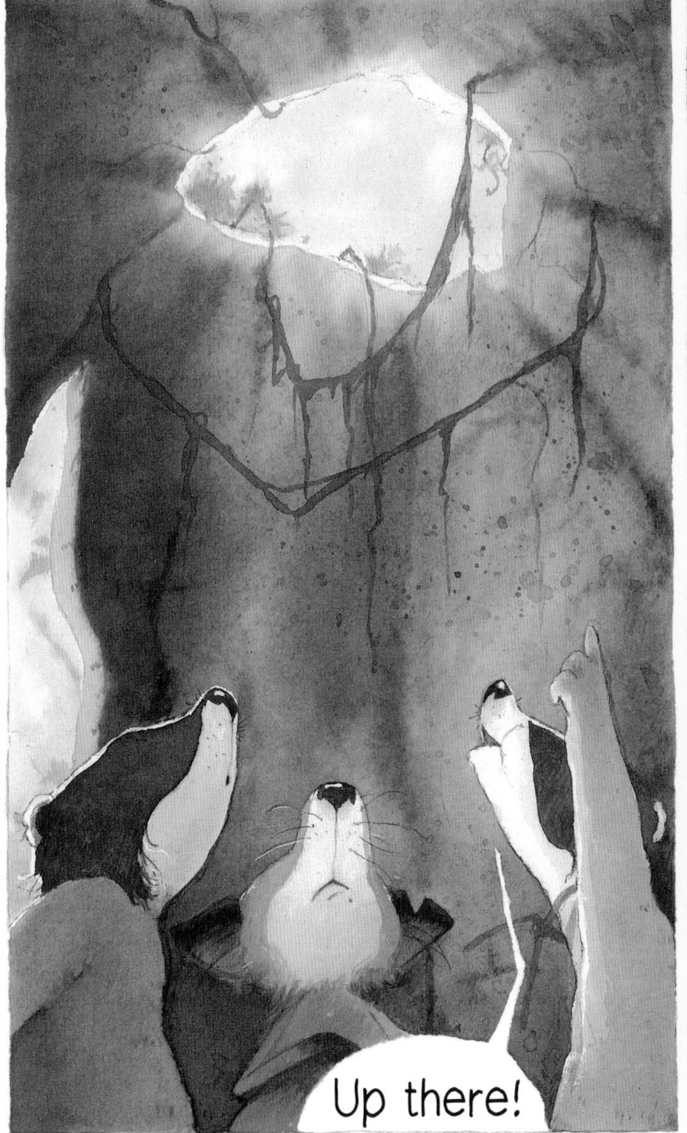
Up there!

But we're not **birds,** Bristle!
We don't need to **fly** to get up there.

All we need are ropes and nets!

All set!
It's very comfy.
But I'm getting hungry. It must be **dinnertime.**
Yikes! It's **late!**
They might start eating without us!
Hurry up. Let's go!
Wait. We have to hide the door, or someone will find our secret clubhouse!
We'll come back after dinner. Come on, Ginger, hurry, or we'll get yelled at!
And a cold meal!
Oh, you and your **dinnertime!** My mother and I always ate whenever we felt like it.

Sorry!
Well, look who showed up!

Why are you late?
We didn't realize what time it was.
And...and there was a dog too.

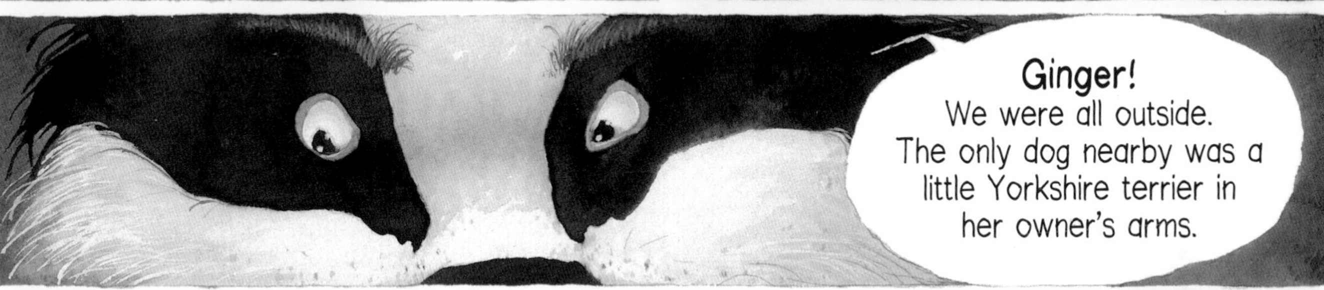
Ginger!
We were all outside. The only dog nearby was a little Yorkshire terrier in her owner's arms.

Yes, true, but you always say we can never be too careful with dogs.

Since you can't get home on time, you'll stay inside after dinner.
But we still have something important to do!

Why, yes, you do, Ginger. And that something is called Cleaning Your Rooms!

What's the matter, Ginger?
Why aren't you cleaning?

You never made me do it before! And I liked it that way. So why do I have to clean up now?

It was just the two of us, before.
Now, there are six of us. It would be a mess if no one picked up after themselves.

Besides, you've known since morning that you had to do it. Tomorrow is **spring cleaning,** so we have to straighten up first.

Toys all gone!
Well done, Berry! You're a good cleaner.

We never had **spring cleaning** before!

Let's just say that badgers are a bit tidier than foxes.
But don't worry. It won't hurt!
Come on now, Ginger. **Get to work!**
Stop being such a goody two-shoes!
She's MY mother!
Aw, darn it!
Fine! So, you want to help me clean, Berry?

Hey!
Psst!
What are you doing?
Can't you tell? I'm waking up your brother.
Is there something scary here?
Nothing scares you, does it?
You bet there is! You should never wake a sleeping badger!

Oh... sorry.
But now that you're both awake, we might as well do something.
Our clubhouse is waiting. We have a job to finish.

I don't believe this!
Come on, Grub! A little night walk and a little adventure never hurt anybody!
Yeah, it's going to be a great adventure when Papa catches us!

If your dad catches us, you can always say I made you do it. He's mean to me anyway, so it won't matter.
When was he ever mean to you?

He's always scolding me.
You're mixing up **mean** and **strict.**
No, believe me. He doesn't like me very much.

What's the matter?
Didn't you hear that?

Berry!!
Why aren't you in bed?
Not sleepy!
Great...now what? Bring her along?
She'll wake up the grown-ups.
We'd better bring her. We won't be long. She won't bother us.
I still feel like someone's watching.
Scaredy-cat! With a moon like this, there's nothing to be scared of.
who-hoo-WHOO!

It's just an owl! She won't hurt us. We're too big for her.
Wait!
Now I can feel it too!

Just think, I could be safe and warm in bed!
We should turn back. I don't want Berry to get too scared.
Pfff! You act like you've never been out at night.

flap flap flap
flap flap flap
OK! Let's go home!

Not so fast, kids!

Relax! Don't tell me you were scared!

Papa!

If it isn't the prettiest little fox of them all!

Papa, meet Berry, Bristle, and Grub.
Good evening, everyone!
Evening!

Where are you going?
To our clubhouse.
Will you come with us?

What are you doing here, Papa?
I just came back from the mountains. I was going to visit you tomorrow.
But how did you find me?
Your mother left a message near the old den.

Oh, no! Someone's here!
I told you we should have covered the door!

No way! We're not going to let a couple of cats bully us!

Hey! What are you doing up there?

What do you want?
That's **our** clubhouse!
Oh yeah? **Says who?**

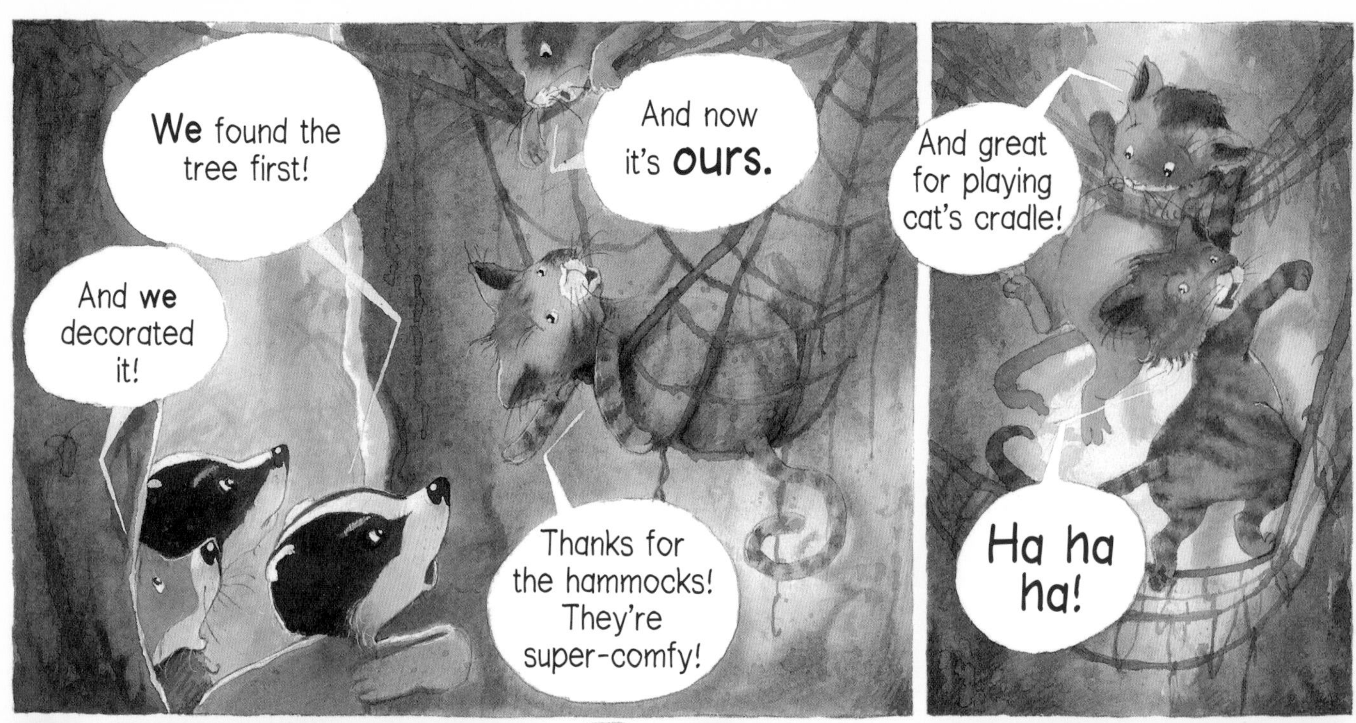
We found the tree first!
And we decorated it!
And now it's ours.
Thanks for the hammocks! They're super-comfy!
And great for playing cat's cradle!
Ha ha ha!

Stop it, or you'll wreck everything!

So what?
Who's going to stop us?

I will, for one.

Oh. OK.

Oh well. Too bad it's so late.
It's so late, we have to go back to the village now.

We'll sort this out next time!

It's lucky you were here! But what if they come back?

They're just two spoiled village cats. As long as you kids stick together, you won't have any trouble.

Now, I'll show you how to hide the door to your excellent clubhouse.
Or else you'll get more unwelcome visitors.

And then I'll take you home to your burrow.

A day without Ginger feels weird.
It's just like her to have fun with her father and leave us with all the chores.

Her dad is so cool, isn't he? When he came to pick her up, he didn't say a word about last night.
Shh!

Last one! Is everything OK?
Yes...
We were just wondering where Ginger's father lives.

He lives everywhere and nowhere. He likes discovering new places. He never stays put.

Maybe that's why they're not together anymore.
Maybe. Anyway, it can't be easy for Ginger.

But she said it also has its good parts.

Now her mother and father don't argue anymore.

And when her dad isn't on his travels...
...he comes to see her every week for a whole day.
So now they almost do more things together than before.

OOPS! Sorry!
Splash
Hey!

We should do something together too...

A water fight!!

There. All clean! Even the children!
Now it's time to dry off the furniture with willow leaves.
Edmund! We've been working so hard! We deserve a break.
How about a picnic while the furniture dries in the air?
Please, Papa!
You're right. We deserve a reward.

Ever since Marguerite started living with us, Papa has become a lot more cool.
For sure.
He would never have left a job unfinished before.
Now he has something else he'd rather do...
...spend time with Marguerite!
Of course! She's so nice!
Yes, she **is** nice!
Why don't we make her a little surprise?

Good-bye, sweetie! I'll be back soon!
I'll show you all my new paintings!

If you're up to no good, don't get caught!
You can count on me!

Careful, darling. The table is going to move.
For Mama!

Thank you, sweetie!

Papa?

She's **my** mother!

Right! **No one** misses me! My father is gone again. My mother has lots of other kids.

It's almost like I don't have any parents at all.

Crack

Hey, look who's here! Our friend from last night. She's all alone, poor thing!
Maybe she won't be so high and mighty now!

Injer!
I'm going to take a short walk with Berry. She won't stay still.
Don't worry about Ginger. Her father will bring her back soon.
Wait for me, Berry. **Where are you going?**
Injer?!
Up here!
Edmund! Berry! **I'm up here!**
What happened to you?
Some cats wanted to take over our clubhouse!

They left to find something to eat. But they said they'd be back!
Oh, no!
Look! They even ruined my painting!
It looks like I'll have to take care of those cats!
They have to learn that they can't pick on one of my children!
You're going to fight them?
No. If you can avoid fighting, you should. You always risk getting hurt. Or hurting someone else, which isn't much better.
Believe me, Ginger. Every fight you avoid is one you win.
But that doesn't mean we have to let others push us around!
We're going to make a little surprise for them. It will teach them to respect others' clubhouses.
Will you help me, Ginger?
You bet!

Fooey! Hunting is too hard around here!
I don't know what mice eat around here. The ones in the village are a lot plumper.
And slower!

I'm going to take a mega-nap! We'll take care of that fox later.
Hey, was the hammock there before?
Move! This hammock looks comfy!

Wait! Something's wrong...

Clunk
Splish
Splash

The next time you say we should come to the forest...
...I'll pull your whiskers out!

They didn't even know what hit them!
And it's better that way. Now they won't want to get back at you.
Edmund?
Did you really mean what you said, before?
What did I say?
You said that I'm one of your children.
That's true. I do think of you as my child.
The proof is that I'm as strict with you as I am with my boys.
I hope it doesn't bother you.
No, not really! But...
Why are you so strict with your children?
I suppose it's because I'm a badger.

If we'd all been there, we'd have given those rotten cats a good beating!
It's easy to be brave now! You never got a good look at their claws!
Don't worry. They got what was coming to them!
It's been a long day, children. Time for bed.
Good night, sweetie.
Mama? Don't you think you have **a lot** of kids now?
Yes! So much the better, right?

And no matter what...
...you'll always be **MY Ginger,** right?

Yes!

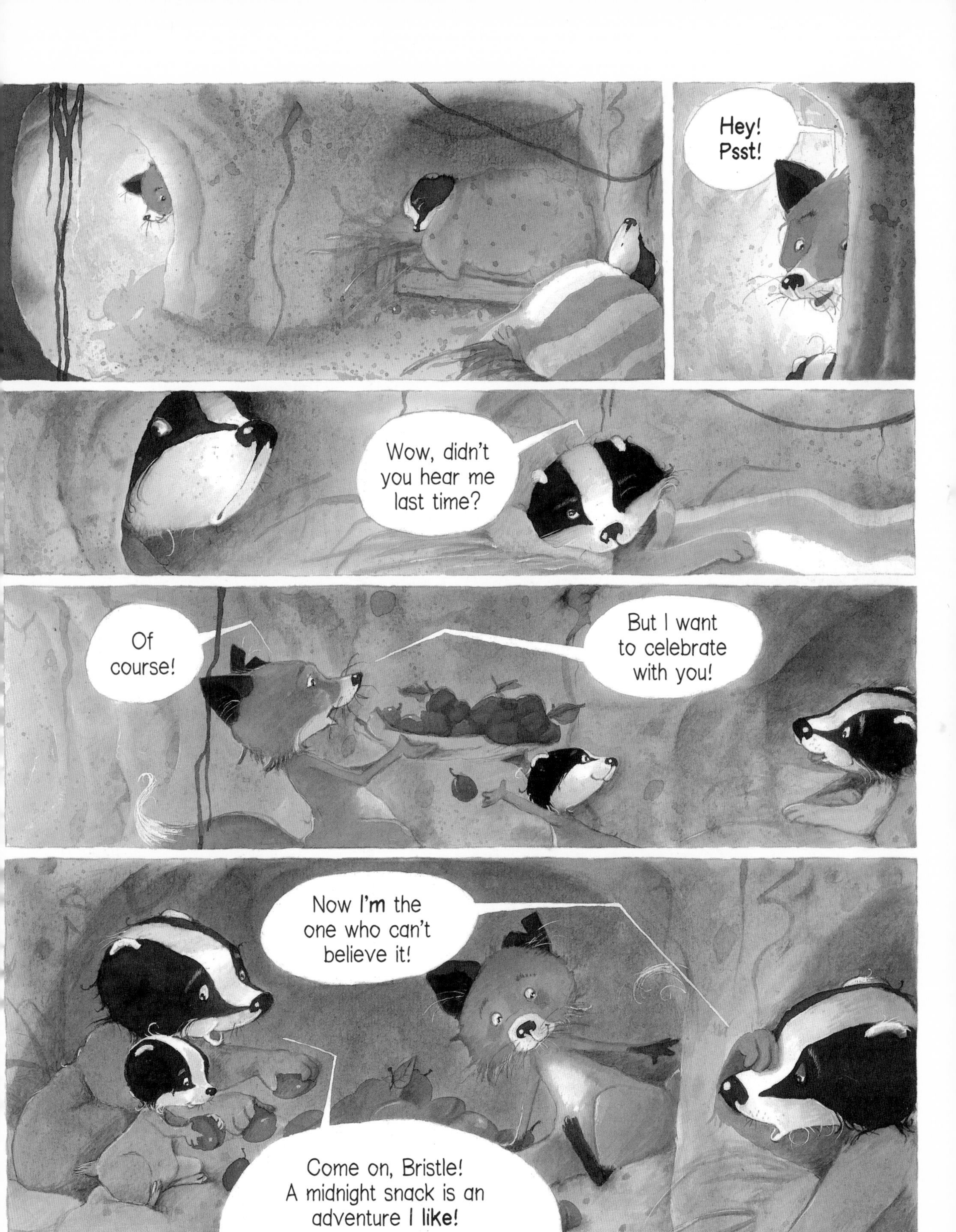
Hey!
Psst!
Wow, didn't you hear me last time?
Of course!
But I want to celebrate with you!
Now **I'm** the one who can't believe it!
Come on, Bristle! A midnight snack is an adventure I **like**!

So, that's what we're celebrating?
I have so many parents!
I'm not so sure it's a good thing, but we also have...
...a lot of **brothers and sisters!**
Hey! Ha!
Time for the second lesson!
Hey, we didn't finish teaching Ginger yet!
You were certainly right, Edmund.
They never get bored when they're together!